Evie's Magic Bracelet

Read more in the Evie's Magic Bracelet series!

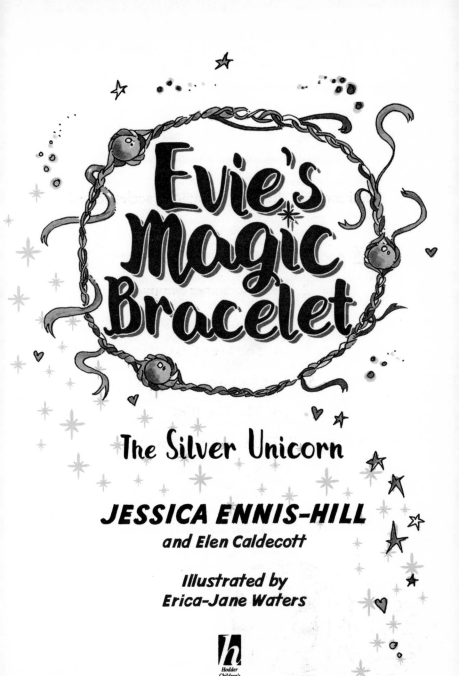

Evie's Magic Bracelet

The Silver Unicorn

JESSICA ENNIS-HILL
and Elen Caldecott

Illustrated by
Erica-Jane Waters

Hodder
Children's
Books

HODDER CHILDREN'S BOOKS

First published in Great Britain in 2017 by Hodder and Stoughton

3 5 7 9 10 8 6 4 2

A CIP catalogue record for this book
is available from the British Library.

ISBN 978 1 444 93439 7

Printed and bound in Great Britain
by Clays Ltd, St Ives Plc

The paper and board used in this book
are made from wood from responsible sources

MIX
Paper from
responsible sources
FSC® C104740

Hodder Children's Books
An imprint of
Hachette Children's Group
Part of Hodder and Stoughton
Carmelite House
50 Victoria Embankment
London EC4Y 0DZ

An Hachette UK Company
www.hachette.co.uk

www.hachettechildrens.co.uk

To Mum, Dad & Carmel: thank you for so many great childhood memories. I hope I can create lots of amazing ones for Reggie to look back on xx – J.E-H.

To Biff – E.C.

Chapter 1

'Evie!' Mum called up the stairs. 'We'll be heading out in fifteen minutes, are you set?'

Evie Hall was sitting on the end of her tidily made bed. She was staring at her carefully laced school shoes – and she was totally panicking.

What if her new school was full of bullies

and monsters? What if the teachers were meaner than a crocodile with a cold? What if all the other pupils ignored her?

Worse. What if they noticed her?

Her heart thumped like a brass band in a washing machine.

'Evie! Are you listening, love?'

She had to be brave. She had to pick up her book bag and stand up. Even though her legs felt like they'd turned to warm plasticine. There was no way she could just stay on her bed for the whole day, however much she wanted to. She had already double- and triple-checked that she had her pencil case and Nana Em's phone number in case of emergencies. She was set. Except for the plasticine leg problem, of course.

Luna, Evie's silver-grey cat, meowed loudly, and leapt on to her lap. Her claws dug like needles, prodding Evie to move.

'Ow! OK, OK, I'm going,' Evie said.

Luna gave a happy purr and stepped on to the bed, where she promptly curled up into a ball. She clearly considered her job done.

'It's all right for you,' Evie said. 'You can spend all day snoozing, you don't have to start at a new school.'

Luna shut her eyes. Snoozing was her favourite.

Evie picked up her book bag and tramped downstairs.

Mum was in the hall, pulling a brush

through her hair. Evie could hear Dad
trying to get her little sister Lily to eat-
her-breakfast-not-play-with-it. Lily was
mithering as usual.

There were still cardboard boxes piled
beside the front door. They hadn't been
unpacked from the move.

Evie was about to ask Mum one last time
whether she really, really, really had to
change schools, just because they'd moved
house, and her old school was miles away,
and they-had-been-through-this-already,
when the doorbell rang.

The postman stood on the doorstep.
'Welcome to Javelin Street!' he said
cheerfully, as he handed a parcel to Mum.

'Thanks!' Mum replied brightly. 'We love it here, don't we, Evie?'

Evie said nothing. She *liked* it here, because they were much closer to Nana Em and Grandpa – next door, in fact. And she had her own room in the attic and didn't have to share with Lily. Which was good because Lily was annoying: she was five and thought the sky was blue because it had rain in it. But *liking* it here wasn't at all the same thing as *loving* it – the one huge, ginormous thing it was missing was her old friends.

'Oh!' Mum looked at the wrapper on the parcel. 'It's for you, Evie.'

For her? She never got parcels. Except on her birthday, which wasn't for ages.

Her tummy did an excited flip, instead of a terrified one. She took the parcel from Mum and cradled it curiously. What was it? Who was it from?

Mum was still chatting to the postman, so Evie slipped into the front room. It was the good room, with the red settee that Myla the dog wasn't allowed to sit on and shed her fur all over. She wanted somewhere quiet – which meant away from Lily – to open the parcel.

It was square, and fitted comfortably between her palms. Pink wrapping paper was held in place with jewel-coloured blue and green ribbons. Her name was written in looped handwriting across the

front. Handwriting that Evie recognised –
Grandma Iris! She lived a long way away
in Jamaica, but she often wrote letters and
cards to her granddaughters. Today she had
sent something really special.

Evie tugged the ribbon free and let the
paper fall. Inside was a box, made of white
card with a red lid. She lifted the lid, her
fingers tingling with excitement.

There, nestled inside soft tissue paper, was
a bracelet. Evie's breath caught. Grandma
Iris had sent her a present, just when she
was feeling low. She lifted it out carefully.
The bracelet twinkled in the dust motes
that danced in shining sunlight. Tightly
plaited silks criss-crossed in colourful

streams. There were beads too, exactly the same silvery-grey colour as Luna's fur. It was beautiful. Evie noticed a small card resting on top of the tissue paper, written by Grandma Iris. 'Good luck at your new school,' it said. 'Have a magical time!'

Magical? School? Ha! There was more chance of pigs putting on an acrobatic aerial show than of having a magical time on her first day. Still, Evie felt warm knowing that Grandma Iris was thinking of her.

She slipped the bracelet on – it fitted perfectly, as though it had been made just for her. For a second, Evie could almost feel Grandma Iris' arms around her in a tight hug. The sun seemed to shine more brightly

through the lace curtains. She felt a tear
in her eye, and the sunbeam shattered into
kaleidoscope shards of gold sparkles.

'Evie,' Mum stuck her head into the room,
'I'll walk you and Lily there. All set?'

Evie blinked and pulled her sleeve down quickly. She knew Mum wouldn't let her wear jewellery to school, but she wanted to keep the warm feeling with her for as long as she could. She pushed the bracelet high up her arm.

Myla bounded into the room. She was

panting and her tongue lolled. It looked exactly like a big grin. She woofed excitedly.

'Myla wants to walk with us,' Evie said, sure that she was right.

Mum laughed. 'Does she now? Well, I'm not stopping every thirty seconds to sniff lamp-posts. We're in a rush! Perhaps tomorrow, Myla.'

Myla stopped grinning. She looked the way Lily did when she got mardy and stuck out her bottom lip.

'Sorry, Myla,' Evie said. She patted the dog's head. 'But what Mum says goes.'

'That's right,' Mum agreed. 'And this mum says it's time for you to start your new school. Let's go.'

Chapter
2

Starrow Junior School was across the busy
High Street. Cars, vans and buses growled
past like metal beasts.

'*I* want to press the button!' Lily wailed,
at the crossing.

Evie shrugged. The closer they got to
school, the heavier her feet felt. Lily could

press the green man today.

'Hold my hand while we cross,' Mum said.

Normally, Evie might roll her eyes; she was old enough to cross on her own. But today was a Day of Doom. So she took Mum's hand – and didn't let go, not even when they were safely on the other side.

The school was old, with dark stone walls that made it look exactly like an ogre's fortress. Apart from all the children, that was. Any ogres would probably eat children, and there were loads of them here running about uneaten. Dozens of children of all different shapes and sizes whizzed past. Evie felt herself leaning closer to Mum: she hated big crowds, especially if there was any chance they were looking at her.

'Do you want me to come in with you?' Mum asked softly, squeezing Evie's hand.

Evie pulled herself up straighter. She had to be brave, even though it felt as if her legs might buckle like wet cardboard. 'No,' she said. 'I can do it.'

'Good girl,' Mum said and dropped a quick kiss on the top of her head. 'I'll take Lily round to the infants. Nana Em will be here at the end of the day. OK?'

Evie let go of Mum and yanked the straps of her book bag higher on her shoulders. She could do this. Probably.

Inside, the school smelled of cooked

dinners. A small boy with tears on his
cheeks and a cut on his knee sat on a blue
chair in reception. A friendly-looking
woman, her hair covered by a black scarf,
pressed a plaster over the graze.

'Hello,' Evie whispered to the woman.

16

She hadn't meant to whisper. She tried again. 'Hello,' she squeaked. This wasn't going well.

'Hello,' the woman replied with a smile.

'I'm new. I'm Evie Hall. Year 6.'

'Lovely! I'm a bit stuck sticking Ollie here, for the minute. But if you go through those doors, turn left, then left, you'll see the Year 6 class on your right. OK?'

Evie nodded. She pushed open the heavy double-doors and found herself in a corridor with a shiny wooden floor and brick walls covered with a chequerboard of drawings and paintings.

Turn left, left, right.

Or was it right, right, left?

Her head flicked from side to side, her feet felt stuck to the ground. Which was it?

'Are you all right?' a voice asked behind her.

She turned and saw a girl with long dark hair and brown eyes. She was almost exactly the same height as Evie. Was she the same age?

'I'm looking for the Year 6 class,' Evie managed to say.

The girl pressed her lips together, as though she were deciding what to do. Her head tilted to one side. 'I'm in Year 6,' she said, eventually.

'Can you tell me where to go?'

Suddenly the girl broke into a huge grin.

'Only if you can keep up!' she said. Without another word, she sprinted to the left, her hair flying like a superhero cape behind her. 'Race you!' she yelled over her shoulder.

Were they allow to run in the corridors? Would she get told off?

The girl was almost out of sight.

She had no choice. She couldn't stand here like a bowl of lemons all day.

Evie took a deep breath, and ran. Her arms swung, her legs stretched out, pounding after the girl. Her footsteps echoed off the walls and she felt herself smiling for the first time since she'd left the house. She was gaining on the girl!

Left again.

Then, she crashed into the girl's back.
They both tumbled to the ground outside
a classroom, in a tangle of arms, legs
and bags.

Oof!

'Isabelle Carter!' an adult voice snapped.
'What on earth are you doing?'

'Sorry, Miss Williams,' the girl replied,
pulling Evie to her feet.

Isabelle winked at Evie and slipped into
the classroom.

Evie followed quickly. Had she made
a friend? Would Isabelle let Evie sit next
to her?

Oh.

Inside the classroom, Isabelle seemed to

have forgotten all about Evie. She had taken a seat next to a cool-looking blond boy and was whispering with him.

Evie dropped her head to her chest. Her grin, gone.

'You must be Evie Hall,' Miss Williams said. 'Welcome to Starrow Juniors. Find yourself a seat. Don't do everything Isabelle Carter tells you to. In fact, if you want my advice, don't do *anything* Isabelle Carter tells you to.'

Evie slid into a seat near the window. Seagulls cawed crossly to one another beneath armour-grey clouds. Evie kept her head down for the rest of the morning and tried to say as little as she possibly could.

She was like a spy in enemy territory: watch, learn, and try to make it out in one piece.

After dinner – her favourite butties eaten on her own in a noisy hall – she rushed out into the yard in relief. It was good to be outdoors. For a while, she stood by herself, watching everyone playing.

'Catch!' Isabelle yelled suddenly. Evie brought her hands up just in time to stop a netball slamming hard into her tummy.

'Good reflexes!' said the blond boy, whose name was Ryan.

Evie threw the ball to him. He bounced it a few times, then took it racing towards a hoop.

'Quick! Stop him!' Isabelle cried.

It was all the encouragement Evie needed. She raced to get between Ryan and the hoop. Isabelle whooped a war cry and leapt into the air. She caught Ryan's shot and slammed the ball home herself.

'Hey! Pack it in! We were playing first!' cried a group of smaller kids with a skipping rope.

'Sorry!' Ryan grabbed the ball and ran to the other end of the yard. Isabelle and Evie were right on his tail.

'You're fast, Evie!' Isabelle said, between gasps.

Evie felt a small tingle of pleasure.

'We're running in a charity paper chase on Wednesday. You should sign up too,' Ryan said, launching the ball at a spare hoop.

'She's probably too late to join in. There were forms and everything,' Isabelle said.

'She could ask,' Ryan replied.

'What's a paper chase?' Evie asked.

24

Ryan caught the ball and bounced it. 'Someone is the hare, they set off first and leave a trail of torn paper. The runners have to follow the paper and the first runner back to the start wins. I'm going to be the hare.'

'But it's after school,' Isabelle said, 'so the forms had to be back ages ago.'

'Oh,' Evie said. 'Oh well. It's OK.' She didn't want to be any bother. She twisted Grandma Iris' bracelet around her wrist distractedly, once, twice, three times. Gold sunlight burst from behind grey clouds.

A loud, insistent bell rang out across the yard.

'Last one back is a stinkbomb!' Isabelle cried. She and Ryan dashed towards the

25

door neck and neck.

'You're a massive stinkbomb, Isabelle!' she heard Ryan shout.

Evie walked back slowly. Isabelle and Ryan had obviously been friends forever. She was just some kid who'd turned up at their school. She was nothing special.

'Move! Move! Move!'

She looked up, to where the rude shouting was coming from. An angry-looking seagull cawed at her. She jumped out of its way as it dived on to an abandoned crisp.

Not even the seagulls wanted her around.

'Mine! Mine! Mine!' another gull cawed at the first.

What?

Evie stared at the squabbling birds. Their caws were getting angrier as the crisp flipped up in the air.

'Me! Me! Me!'

'Mine! Mine!'

Evie leaned in closer. She could understand their caws. She knew what the noises meant.

But that wasn't possible. It just wasn't.

She moved closer. Their yellow eyes and red-tipped beaks looked mean. 'Excuse me, but—'

She stopped herself.

This was her very first day at a brand-new school. Did she really want to be seen talking to seagulls?

'Evie!'

The shout came from above her. She looked up. Was a seagull shouting her *name*?

No. Miss Williams was at the Year 6 window. 'Evie, hurry up now, class is starting again.'

Evie felt her cheeks burn. She must have been imagining things.

Chapter 3

Evie knew it was a terrible idea to spend
the rest of the afternoon gazing out of the
window. Who knew how far behind she
was? She should be taking notes. They might
even study things at Starrow Juniors that
she had never done before, like Japanese, or
knitting, or bagpipes.

But she couldn't get the seagulls out of her head. She really, really wanted one to fly close enough to be able to hear it. The seagulls hadn't seemed friendly. But she needed to know – could she really understand their calls? The birds swooped and circled without ever coming near.

When the bell went at the end of the day, Evie joined the stream of children heading out to the yard. There was Nana Em! Oh, and there was Lily too.

'Evie, how was your day, petal?' Nana Em pulled Evie into a warm hug.

'I'm not sure,' Evie said. It was important to be truthful.

'OK,' Nana Em said, 'I know what we

should do. The city farm is just around the corner from the school. Let's go and visit before we head home. That will raise your spirits.'

Yes!

The city farm was perfect. She could listen to all the animals then, and see if she could understand them too.

They walked past the greengrocer, smelling of summer; the newsagents with the patchwork of adverts in the window; the pizza delivery place with the bustling crowd at the counter. The High Street was busy.

The farm was busy too – there were lots of children in Starrow Juniors uniform,

though she didn't know any of them. Nana
Em pointed out ducklings dunking on the
pond, and squirrels leaping from branch
to branch.

Evie lagged further and further behind

as Lily and Nana Em walked excitedly around the farm.

There was a horse paddock, just beyond the petting area. Evie stopped there and lifted herself up on to the fence. The wood felt warm under her fingertips. Grandma Iris' lovely bracelet slid down and rested on the back of her hand. She twisted it around her wrist. Once, twice, three times.

The sun glittered golden on the back of her hand. Gold light splashed across her wrist. It was almost as if ...

'Evie?' The voice came from behind her. It was Ryan, from school. He swung himself up on to the fence. 'I thought it was you. Are you watching out for Snowy?'

He nodded towards the paddock.

'Who's Snowy?'

'He's Snowy.' Ryan pointed to a horse who was standing beneath a tree. He was white, with speckled grey spots on his flank. His head was down and his tail was still. He didn't look well.

'What's up with him?' Evie asked.

'I don't know. I come here most days after school, and usually Snowy comes over and says hello. But today ...' Ryan trailed off.

Suddenly, Snowy leapt into the air as if he'd been bitten. He gave a yelp, then cantered in a tight circle. He kicked up dust in a red cloud.

'Snowy?' Ryan sounded worried. 'Snowy,

what's the matter, boy?'

'You should get someone. A vet, or something!' Evie said.

Ryan jumped down from the fence and dashed towards the farm building.

Snowy was neighing desperately. 'Nooho! Nooho!'

'What is it, Snowy? Tell me!' Evie wasn't expecting Snowy to reply.

But that is exactly what he did.

'Now! Ouch,' the horse whinnied. 'No! Ho! No!'

Evie could understand Snowy's whickers and whinnies. She could understand Horse! She gripped the fence tighter.

'What hurts, Snowy?'

'Nasty ninnies,' Snowy said. 'Nibbling, nipping. Naughty!'

Evie heard high-pitched giggles coming from the horse's flank.

'Who's naughty?' she asked. The giggling got louder.

'Nooo!' Snowy bucked again.

'Gentle, gentle,' Evie soothed. 'Let me see.'

He stopped kicking and stomping for a second. The dust settled. And Evie saw exactly what was bothering Snowy.

On his back were two creatures, small, not even as big as dolls. The creatures were blue, with fine wings and long legs.

What were they?

Not butterflies. They were way too big.

Not birds. They had no feathers.

Nana Em had read her a book of folk tales once that had delicate, painted illustrations. These creatures reminded her of those illustrations.

The word 'sprites' popped into her head.

Really? Sprites?

First seagulls spoke and now creatures out
of a folk tale had sprung up in a city farm.

This was *not* what she'd expected from
her first day of school.

But she had no time to wonder. Snowy
was in trouble. The sprites were hurting him
– they were his 'nasty ninnies'! Well. There
was no way she was going to stand for that.
Before she could even think twice, Evie
found herself clambering over the fence and
stomping towards the horse.

'Hey, sprites!' she cried. 'You leave Snowy
alone.'

The two sprites jerked upright. They let
Snowy's tail go. 'You can see us?' she heard
a high-pitched voice shriek.

'I can see you, and I'm telling you to leave Snowy be! What has he ever done to you?'

The second sprite laughed. 'The little girl thinks she can tell us what to do! Hee hee.'

The bigger of the two blue sprites flittered its wings and rose sharply into the air. 'Nobody tells sprites what to do. Not ever!' it yelled.

Then it twirled in the air, its wings buzzing quickly. Evie noticed its sharp little nails, its narrowed eyes. She saw it hold its pinching fingers towards her. And then, it flew!

As fast as a dart, it hurtled towards her. The second one whooped and launched itself too.

She turned and ran! She had never run so fast before in her life. Her legs were like pistons, pounding up and down, her body leaning into the wind. She moved as though a lion were chasing her. The fence was getting closer, closer, closer …

She hit the top with her right hand and sprang right over it, like a gymnast. As soon as her feet hit the ground, she dropped into a ball. She heard two pairs of buzzing wings sail over, yelling and whooping. Then, the sound faded, as they flew on.

'Wow!' Ryan's voice said. 'I've never seen anyone jump a fence like that. You cleared it with room to spare. You should really take part in the paper chase, you know.

You'd be brilliant.'

Evie nodded, but she wasn't really listening. A horse had spoken. And a seagull. And even Myla had seemed a bit odd that morning when she had opened Grandma Iris' present.

Grandma Iris.

All this had started as soon as she put on the bracelet!

'Ryan,' Evie said, 'I have to go. I have to get home. I'll see you in school tomorrow. OK? I think Snowy is feeling a bit better now.'

With that she raced to find Nana Em and Lily – she had some investigating to do!

Chapter 4

Evie found Nana Em and Lily near the café, arguing over the number of treats Lily had already eaten that day and how an ice cream would spoil her tea. It sounded as though Lily was winning.

'Can we go home?' Evie asked. 'I need to get back to ... eh ...' She couldn't even begin to explain. Who would believe her if she told them what had happened?

But Nana Em just smiled. 'I suppose you have had a long day, chick. Home it is.'

Lily scowled, but gave in.

As soon as they were inside the door, Myla the Labrador rushed to say hello.

'Bow-wowzers!' she huffed joyfully, her tail thumping from side to side. As her tail wagged, bright golden sparks showered around her. Nana Em didn't seem to notice at all!

'Myla!' Evie said. 'Hello!'

Nana Em bustled in through the door to the hall. Lily kicked her shoes off and dropped her coat on the floor. Evie got squished right up against the cardboard boxes.

'On the hook, Lily!' Nana Em warned. 'There's too many of us in here. Myla, out! Go in the garden.'

'Garden!' Myla barked and thudded excitedly towards the kitchen.

Evie was just about to run after Myla, to hear what else she had to say, but then she remembered the parcel.

She dashed into the front room and flipped the cushions aside on the settee. Where was it? She'd left it right here. There! The pink paper was crushed and the ribbons drooped. The white box with its red lid had tipped on its side.

Evie tugged off the lid and riffled through the tissue paper until she found the note. On one side was the message she remembered: Good luck at your new school. Have a magical time! She flipped it over – and saw there was a message on the back too! She'd missed it earlier.

> All that glitters isn't gold,
> Uncover magic, be brave, be bold.
> Its power wanes on the third day.
> Bark! Woof! Howl! What will you say?

Uncover magic? Barking and woofing? Evie let the note flutter back into the box and she sat down with a heavy *whump* on the settee. Grandma Iris had sent her a magic bracelet. Grandma Iris had sent her a MAGIC bracelet! She pulled back the sleeve of her sweatshirt and looked at her wrist.

The tightly woven threads looked so pretty. The grey stones glittered. She twisted it around her wrist. One, twice, three times.

As she stared, a thin trail of gold light swirled in the centre of the stones. It circled and spiralled, getting brighter and brighter. Then, it twisted out of the stones, snaking a path along the bracelet. Soon, the band of gold was dancing around her wrist – a trail of bright glitter! Evie felt her heart thump harder than Myla's tail. Then, just as soon as it had appeared, the light vanished.

Wow.

She had just seen magic. Not a party trick, or special effects. Real live magic! It was impossible. It was wonderful.

Evie found herself giggling. Then laughing. Then she leapt up off the settee and danced something that was halfway

48

between a jig and a breakdance. 'Thank you, Grandma Iris!' she yelled.

'What was that, chick?' Nana Em's voice came from the back kitchen.

'Nothing!' Evie said, hugging herself in delight. There was no way she could tell anyone – no one would believe her. This was a gift just for her.

She pulled down her sleeve.

The gold light was gone completely. She remembered the note: 'All that glitters isn't gold'. Was that gold light magical? Was that what Grandma Iris meant? It would have been so much easier if Grandma had written a proper explanation, not a poem! But that wasn't Grandma Iris' way. She liked puzzles and riddles. Well, so did Evie. And she was going to work this puzzle out.

She was going to hunt for magic. Starting with Myla, and Luna the cat.

Myla was still out in the back garden with Lily – she could hear the shrieks as Lily bounced on her trampoline. Perhaps Luna was upstairs?

In the hallway, Evie stopped. One of the cardboard boxes was open and she could see a soft glow, like a nightlight, coming from inside. A soft, *golden* glow. She lifted the brown flap and peered inside.

She could see framed photographs – Mum's plan was to put them up on the stairs, so that everyone would see them on

50

their way up. There were photos of Lily and Evie when they were babies, photos of Mum and Dad smiling together, photos of Nana Em and Grandpa on their wedding day, and Grandma Iris too. Gold light ran, almost like water flowing, around the frames. It was beautiful. Evie reached out to touch it, but it darted away from her fingertips. She let the lid lower.

Evie trotted up the stairs.

Luna was curled up, fast asleep on Evie's bed. Evie woke her gently. 'Luna,' she whispered, 'Luna, can you hear me?'

Luna arched her back, stretching her legs, yawned, and purred, 'Is it time for breakfast?'

'I can understand you!' Evie gasped.

'Good,' Luna replied. 'Shall we see if there's any tuna?'

Luna leapt neatly on to the floor and stepped, like a dancer, out of the room.

'Luna! Wait!'

Luna had already padded her way downstairs. Evie followed. In the narrow kitchen, Luna was winding her way in and out of Nana Em's ankles, purring loudly. Under the deep purr, Evie could hear Luna say, 'Fish, pretty please. Fish, pretty please.'

'Luna!' Nana Em said. 'Get out from under my feet!' She swooped Luna up and dropped her outside the back door. The cat stalked away, her tail high in the air like an indignant exclamation mark. 'Tea will be ready in five minutes, Evie.' Nana Em turned back to the stove. She stirred a saucepan of spaghetti and hummed a song. It was her favourite, about flying to the

moon and playing among stars. As Nana
Em sang, Evie noticed the strangest thing.
Little sparks of gold glitter seemed to
shower around her like miniature fireworks.
More magic!

She was working this out. Maybe magic
appeared when nice things happened? And
perhaps Grandma Iris had taken some of
that magic and put it in a bracelet for her
to use? What had the note said? 'Its power
wanes on the third day.' She wondered if
Grandma Iris had given her just enough
magic to be able to understand animals for
three days?

Evie felt as though she had her own
fireworks exploding inside her. What a

wonderful thing Grandma Iris had done!

She ate her tea at the table, smiling to herself. She hugged Mum and Dad extra specially hard when they got home from work. She even managed to be nice to Lily for the Whole Evening, even when Lily put her sticky hands on Evie's school uniform. She was too happy to get properly cross. When she was tucked up into bed, and Mum gave her a kiss goodnight, she saw the brightest thread of magic stretch between her cheek and Mum. When her eyes finally closed, she thought how lucky she was to have her family – yes, even Lily.

Chapter 5

Evie slept wearing Grandma Iris' bracelet, and she tucked it under her school sweatshirt the next morning. There was no way she was going to leave it anywhere where Lily's sticky mitts could get close to it. She made her bed and smoothed down the duvet before skipping downstairs.

Dad and Lily were at the table in the dining room. There was a jumble of cereal boxes in front of them. Myla sat beneath the table, her tail thumping on the floor, hoping that Lily's terrible messy eating would send treats raining down on the floor. Dad was reading the news on his phone.

He looked up. 'You look brighter this morning! Yesterday you looked like a wet weekend. Are you looking forward to school?'

Evie gave a huge grin. 'Yes,' she said, 'I am.'

'Good.'

Was the magic still working? She twisted the bracelet beneath her sleeve and saw a burst of gold spark from the dog's thumping tail. 'Lovely Lily!' Myla woofed. 'Lovely Rice Krispos! Lovely food!'

'Hush, Myla,' Dad said, 'it's too early for barking.'

Evie winked at Myla.

Mum walked them to school. Today Evie kept a keen eye out for any sign of magic.

Lily's fingers burst with it when she pressed the green-man button. A trail of magic burst like a jet engine from a boy racing by on a scooter. At the school gates, gentle cloud-bursts of it seemed to settle on parents hugging their kids goodbye.

She remembered the way to the Year 6 classroom without any trouble. Inside, she took the same window seat as yesterday, but she gave Ryan a shy smile on her way past his chair. He nodded in return. Then he nudged Isabelle, who leapt out of her seat and rushed over to Evie.

'Ryan said you were amazing yesterday!' Isabelle said. 'He said you helped Snowy and then jumped a fence like a total superhero.'

Evie felt her cheeks flushing warmly. 'I don't know about that. I just had to get out of the paddock quickly.'

'Why?' Isabelle's head tipped inquisitively.

'Because I was being chased,' Evie said, without thinking.

'By Snowy?'

'No.'

'Who then?' Isabelle asked.

Evie bit her lip. She couldn't say sprites. She couldn't. There was no way that Isabelle would believe her. It was only her second day at school and if she said the word 'sprites' out loud then the whole school would think she was a baby. Or a liar. Or a lying baby. She wanted the floor to open up and swallow her, shoes and all. Isabelle was staring. What could she say? Her mind went blank.

Isabelle frowned. 'Suit yourself,' she said. 'I was going to ask Miss Williams if you could join in the paper chase tomorrow, but I won't bother now.' She turned so sharply her dark hair flicked like Snowy's tail.

Evie slumped into her seat. She wished she could go and apologise to Isabelle, to explain. But how could she? It was impossible.

Miss Williams came in and Evie soon found herself circling the verbs in sentences about cats. But she could hardly concentrate and half of her answers were wrong. She'd circled the word 'cat' more than once.

At break, she dashed into the yard. She wanted to be by herself. Most of the yard was concrete, with the basketball hoops separated by painted lines on the ground. But at the far end there were huge wooden planters full of herbs and climbing flowers. There was a shed too, for storing gardening tools. And for hiding behind when a person had made a complete idiot of herself in front of the only people who'd been nice to her at Starrow Juniors.

The garden planters smelled nice – rosemary and lavender hummed with the sound of bees. They left golden trails, like the vapour of tiny aeroplanes, as they flew from flower to flower. She breathed in gently. Then she heard footsteps heading towards her. Ryan.

'Don't worry about Isabelle,' he said when he got close, 'she likes drama.'

'I didn't mean to be dramatic,' Evie said.

Ryan laughed. 'With Isabelle, *everything* is dramatic. Hey, Isabelle!' he called across to the yard. Isabelle was sitting in sunshine on a low wall. She jumped down and strolled across.

Evie looked down at her shoes.

'What's up?' Isabelle asked.

'I think Evie should sit with us at dinner time.'

Isabelle sniffed. 'Fine. But only if she

tells us what she was running away from. I don't like secrets.'

'You don't like *other people* keeping secrets,' Ryan corrected.

'Same thing,' Isabelle replied. She turned to Evie. Her dark eyes were like mirrors and Evie could see herself reflected back, small and scared.

Should she tell them? Could she? Her palms felt sweaty. Her mouth was dry.

'Well?' Isabelle tapped her foot impatiently.

Evie looked at Ryan, who gave a small nod. 'You can trust us,' he said.

Somehow, she felt as though she could. So, she took a deep breath. She was going to risk it. 'Sprites,' she whispered.

'What?'

'Sprites,' Evie said, a little louder. 'I got a bracelet from my gran and it means I can see magic, and sprites, and I can understand what animals say.'

No one spoke. The yells and shouts of the children playing nearby sounded far away. Ryan and Isabelle both stared at her.

Her face flamed. 'You don't believe me,' Evie said.

'No,' Isabelle replied, 'of course we don't.'

'Isabelle!' Ryan said.

'Well, we don't, do we?' she asked him.

He shrugged apologetically. 'I guess not. But you could be nicer about it.'

'I *am* nice!' Isabelle insisted.

Evie raised her hands. 'It's OK,' she said sadly. 'I didn't think you would believe me, not really. But I didn't want to lie to you either. It's all right. You can think I'm weird, if you want.' She stepped away, heading towards the garden shed. She was probably going to have to get used to the garden shed.

'Wait!' Isabelle said, and reached out to grab Evie's arm.

As Isabelle's hand circled Evie's wrist, she touched the bracelet. Suddenly, gold light snaked out through the fabric of her sweatshirt and wrapped itself around Isabelle's hand.

Could Isabelle see it?

The look of sudden shock and horror and alarm on Isabelle's face made Evie think that she probably could.

'What. Is. That?' Isabelle asked.

68

Yes, she definitely could.

'Ryan! Hold Evie's wrist!' Isabelle demanded.

Ryan did as he was told. The gold light twisted and turned and wrapped itself around his hand too.

'It's magic,' Evie said softly.

'Cool,' Ryan said, his eyes fixed on the light.

'It's real! You were telling the truth.' Isabelle tugged excitedly on Evie's arm. 'And talking to animals, was that true?'

'Yes.'

'And sprites?'

'Yes. But they're mean. We should stay away from them.'

'Did they look like fairies? With silvery wings and cute little dresses?' Isabelle asked.

'No. Well, they had wings. I can't describe them, really. I was too busy trying to get out of their way.'

Isabelle and Ryan let go of her arm, and the golden light faded.

'You know what this means?' Isabelle asked.

'No, what?'

'It means we're going on a sprite hunt!'

Chapter 6

Isabelle's eyes glistened excitedly. 'We have to find a sprite. I really want to see one.'

Evie leaned back against the solid wooden planter. 'But, Isabelle, they're nasty. The two I saw yesterday were tormenting Snowy. They chased after me too.' She wasn't sure she wanted to see a sprite ever again in her whole life, if she could help it.

'How does it work?' Ryan asked, pointing to her wrist.

'I'm not sure. Grandma Iris included a riddle instead of an instruction manual, so I'm trying to work it out.'

'Can you really talk to animals?'

Evie took Isabelle's hand and pulled her closer to the flowers. A fat, furry bee was stumbling from one lavender top to the next. Its buzz was like a hummed song. 'Hazy, lazy, daisy is my favoureeet,' the bee trilled. A slow ribbon of gold floated behind him.

'Can you hear that?' Evie whispered. Isabelle's hand was still grasped in hers.

Isabelle gave a sharp squeeze. 'I can! I can!'

72

The bee lurched off in alarm.

'Oh wait! Come back!' Isabelle said, but the bee soared up and was carried away from the yard on a breeze.

At that moment, the bell rang for the end of break.

'We have to go in,' Ryan said sadly.

'I know. But we should all go to the farm after school,' Isabelle said. 'I want to find a sprite. And I've decided, Evie, I'm going to ask Miss Williams if you can join in the paper chase after all.'

Evie asked Nana Em if she could go to the farm again with Ryan and Isabelle.

'We'll all go,' Nana Em said.

Isabelle slipped her arm through Evie's on the way. As long as they were touching, then Isabelle could see the sparks of magic too. They were getting easier to see now Evie knew what she was looking for – Lily's hand in Nana Em's had a golden halo; a

74

man singing along loudly to a song on his car stereo was surrounded by a mist of golden glitter; a woman pushing a double pram with two rosy twin babies inside had firework bursts of it above her head.

'This is amazing!' Isabelle said. 'You're amazing!'

'It's Grandma Iris, not me,' Evie said.

'Same difference. Hey, Miss Williams said you can do the paper chase!'

Evie felt a little glow that twisted gold in the air in front of them both. Isabelle was her friend! They both giggled.

At the farm, Nana Em took Lily to see the rabbits. Lily mithered a bit because she wanted to stay with Evie and her friends, but

a desperate glance from Evie was enough.
Nana Em whisked Lily away.

'Let's see Snowy!' Ryan said. 'I want to
know what he's thinking.' He broke into a
run and the other two chased after him. At
Snowy's paddock, it was only a second or
two before the horse trotted over to see his
favourite visitor.

'Kind boy!' Snowy whinnied.

'What did he say?' Ryan asked.

Evie was about to tell him. Then she
slipped off her bracelet and handed it to
Ryan. 'Ask him yourself,' she said.

Ryan took it and carefully put it on.
Then he turned to Snowy. 'Hello?' he said.
The horse burst into a string of whinnies

and neighs. But without the bracelet, Evie couldn't understand what he was saying.

Ryan seemed to though. He smiled shyly, then his cheeks turned pink. 'Me too,' he said. He rested his hand on Snowy's nose and stood still for a minute. Then he took off the bracelet and gave it back to Evie. 'Thank you,' he said.

'Do you want a turn?' Evie asked Isabelle.

She nodded eagerly and tugged the bracelet on to her wrist.

'Snowy,' Isabelle said in a very business-like voice, 'do you know where the sprites are? I really want to see them.'

The horse neighed.

'Oh. I see. Thank you.' Isabelle gave the

bracelet back to Evie. 'He says they haven't been back here since you chased them off.'

'I didn't do any chasing!' Evie said.

'Maybe one of the other animals has seen them?' Ryan suggested.

They tried all the animals on the farm – the sheep with her lambs, the pig, the hamsters and rabbits – but nobody could tell them anything. The sprites seemed to have vanished.

Just as they were about to search for Nana Em and head home, a voice hissed at them from behind a wheelie bin. 'Hey, you three.'

'Hello?' Evie said.

A red and white animal slinked out – a fox!

'I hear you're looking for someone,' the fox said. 'I might be able to help.' It turned in the shadow of the bin, checking that the coast was clear, then it tucked itself back into the darkness. 'I heard the sprites have made a home for themselves nearby. But if I tell you where, I want you to open the lid of this bin for me. There's some chips inside that smell delicious.'

Evie told the other two what the fox had said.

'You open the bin, Ryan,' Isabelle said, 'you're the tallest. And I'm not touching a bin, not even for a fox.'

Ryan looked reluctant, but he did as the fox had asked. The stench that rose from the open container was enough to make Evie need to cover her nose. 'Eww!'

'Delicious,' the fox drawled. 'The sprites are camped out in Beau Mount Park.'

'Where?' Evie asked – the park was huge and the sprites were tiny.

'Not near the pond, they hate the water.

Look under the thickest trees. Now, if you'll excuse me, it's time for tea.' He leapt up and scrambled his way into the rubbish, sending up another cloud of stinky air.

'Eww,' Evie said again.

'Did he tell you where they were?'

'Yes,' Evie said. 'But we can't go there now. I have to find Nana Em.'

'Fine,' Isabelle said, 'then tomorrow.'

'We can't tomorrow,' Ryan said, 'it's the paper chase straight after school.'

Isabelle looked determined. She crossed her arms. 'Well,' she said, 'Evie, bring your PE kit. You'll be running in that paper chase, and then we'll go looking for sprites.'

Evie nodded, though she wasn't at all

82

sure that she wanted to search for them. If anything, she wanted never to go near the park again, if there were sprites there.

Before they left, she turned to the bin. 'Thank you, Mr Fox,' she said.

She heard a muffled reply, but the fox had found the chips and was talking with his mouth full, so she couldn't understand.

She hoped she wouldn't regret listening to him.

Chapter 7

As soon as the school bell rang at the end of the following day, Isabelle leapt up from her desk and skipped towards Evie.

'Are you ready to find sprites?' Isabelle asked eagerly.

'I thought it was the paper chase first?' Evie asked. She had told Mum and Dad about the race last night and Dad had promised to finish work early so that he could watch it. She had triple-checked her bag to make sure she had her PE kit.

Isabelle grinned. 'Ryan is going to be the hare! That means that he heads off first with the confetti paper and lays the trail for everyone to follow.'

'Yes, I know,' Evie said, packing up her book bag.

'Evie! That means he can lead the runners into the park, right next to the big trees. We can run the race *and* look for sprites. Both at the same time!'

Evie zipped her bag up slowly. She'd seen the sprites. They were badly behaved. And they liked playing tricks. Was it really a good idea to lead a group of racing children right through the middle of their home? What if the sprites decided to tie everyone's shoe laces together? Or put banana skins on the track?

But Isabelle was so excited.

The sports changing rooms were at the back of the school. Children rushed towards them from all directions. Dark pegs were set into whitewashed brick walls. Hard wooden benches ran below them. Evie got changed slowly. On either side, girls jostled for space. Isabelle talked excitedly the whole time. They were near enough to the yard that Evie could hear the parents and friends and grandparents arriving to watch. The chatter of the crowd was like water rushing over a waterfall. By the time she pulled on her trainers, it was a roar. How many people were there? It sounded like a huge number. She tied her laces slowly. And tightly, in case of sprite attack.

'Ready?' Isabelle asked brightly.

'I don't know,' Evie said.

'You look ready.'

Bursts of magic popped above the excited heads of the girls nearby. But there was no magic at all above Evie's. She felt that any cloud above her head was grey and rain-filled. Perhaps with a bit of thunder in it too.

'What's up?' Isabelle crouched in front of

Evie, with her hands planted on her knees.

'I don't want to go out there,' Evie whispered.

'Why not?'

'There's so many people. I hate big crowds.'

Isabelle gave her a sympathetic look.

'There are a lot of people. But here's the thing: every single one of those people out there wants us to do well. They want to see us try our best, and they will cheer every single runner over the line from the first to the last, because they know that we are all trying our hardest. Are you ready to try your hardest?'

Evie swallowed. She was ready.

Girls had been leaving the changing room, and they were nearly the last. Evie nodded, then stood. She tucked her school shoes neatly under the bench, below her uniform. Her hoodie had long sleeves, so she could tuck her bracelet out of sight. Then she followed Isabelle.

The crowd outside cheered the runners as they stepped out of the building. The mass of people spread right across the yard, as far as the garden shed. It was a bright day and the sun felt warm on her face. She saw a tiny spark of magic flash above her head – more of an indoor sparkler than a proper firework. But it was something. Maybe it was going to be OK after all. She saw Dad's face in the crowd and gave him a shy wave. He yelled her name loud enough to be heard over the din.

Then, she remembered that Ryan was going to lead the runners right through the sprites' den.

The spark puffed out.

Was there anything she could do to stop him?

She looked around. Where was Ryan?

He was right at the far end of the yard, near the gate. His blond hair looked golden in the sunshine and his grin spread like warm honey across his face. He was so happy. Evie noticed a cloth bag slung over his shoulder, stuffed like a Christmas turkey with confetti. He was ready for the race.

Could she make it over to him? Tell him to stay away from the sprites?

Runners in crisp white T-shirts or navy hoodies swarmed in front of her, blocking her view. She squeezed her water bottle anxiously.

'The hare is in position,' Miss Williams shouted over the babbling of the crowd. 'Runners to their marks, if you please.'

Everyone lined up along the edge of the yard, facing the gate. Evie tried to see Ryan, to try to warn him somehow, but she was too small to see. Bodies crowded all around her.

'This is exciting!' Isabelle's voice whispered in her ear. They were together near the back of the runners.

'The hare will run on my first whistle. The runners will go on the second whistle. The hare will complete a circuit of his choice, ending back in the yard. The first runner to reach the yard, behind the hare, will win.'

Miss Williams held a silver whistle to her mouth and gave a sharp blow.

Ryan was off!

It was too late to warn him. She would have to run as fast as she could and hope she reached him before he made it to the sprites. Would she be quick enough?

She had to be.

It was a tense wait. The runners were silent now. Some stretched or jogged on the spot. The parents were still too – all waiting for the second whistle.

Eventually, it came, loud and insistent, and together the runners surged forward.

'Come on!' Isabelle said.

Evie didn't need to be told twice. She

threaded her way through the group, trotting at first, because they were so tightly packed. Once they were out of the gate, the runners picked up the pace. White drifts of paper strips settled on the pavement. She weaved through a pack of serious-looking Year 5 runners. She leapt past some not-at-all-serious Year 3s who had stopped running and seemed to be playing hopscotch instead.

Teachers stood along the road, cheering, and making sure everyone stayed safe.

Ryan was still out of sight though. Evie was sprinting now, with Isabelle right at her elbow. They pulled ahead of the main pack, stretching their lead with every stride.

'You really do want to get to the sprites, don't you?' Isabelle said as they reached Beau Mount Park.

'No,' Evie managed between breaths, 'I just want to keep Ryan safe.'

A flurry of paper whirled and danced around the railings at the park entrance. They followed the narrow path. Banks of green grass rose in hillocks. Hawthorn and elder grew along the path to the right. The pond glistened in the distance.

'There!' Isabelle had seen Ryan's paper trail – headed towards the copse of hawthorns.

And that is when Evie heard Ryan scream.

Chapter 8

Evie and Isabelle's eyes locked. For a
second they froze. Had they really heard
Ryan scream?

The cry came again.

Yes. They had.

It came from the trees. Evie gripped
Isabelle's hand and they pelted together

into the shadows.

'Ryan?' Isabelle called. 'Ryan, where are you?'

The hawthorn bushes were thick, their dark leaves blocked out the sun. A canopy of elder and birch stretched thin twig fingers towards the sky. Underfoot, ancient leaf mould rotted to dust. It smelled damp and the air was cold against Evie's skin. She shivered.

'Ryan?' she called.

'Over here!' His reply was shaky, trembling.

Was it the sprites? Evie and Isabelle inched forward, scared of whatever it was they would discover. Evie thought of the sprites'

cruel laugh – had they hurt Ryan?

The dense twists of trunk and branch thinned suddenly and Evie found that they were in a clearing.

Ryan was there, pressed up against the trunk of a sycamore.

He was staring, wide-eyed, at the thing that had made him scream.

It was huge. Not a sprite at all. A horse. Its silver flank looked ghostly in the gloom. Its brilliant tail flicked in annoyance.

What was a horse doing loose in the park?

Then the horse raised its head and Evie saw, for the first time, that it had an opal-shimmering horn rising from the centre of its forehead.

Not a horse.

'Is that a unicorn?' Isabelle squeaked.

The unicorn – and it was, definitely, a unicorn – whickered and shook his head viciously from side to side. Ryan pressed himself against the tree as the tip of the animal's horn cut through the air in front of him.

Bursts of magic exploded in the air around the unicorn. Instead of the soft golden glow she'd seen so far, this magic looked hot and fierce. The unicorn stamped his hind legs, bucking and kicking out angrily.

Evie and Isabelle crept as close as they could. Ryan caught sight of them and his eyes flashed with hope.

103

'What did you do to the unicorn?' Isabelle said.

'Nothing,' he whispered. 'You have to help me! I can't get past!'

He was right. The rearing unicorn had backed Ryan into a corner, and the tree was too sheer to climb. If he stepped away from its cover, then he was likely to be kicked. The unicorn had him trapped.

'We should get a teacher,' Isabelle said.

Evie was about to do what Isabelle said – they could run back to the school and find a teacher on the way. But how long would that take? And adults might not even be able to see the danger. The creature was getting more and more angry – she could hear his breath coming hard, flaring his nostrils. His eyes rolled wildly.

Evie had seen this before – the unicorn was behaving just like Snowy at the city farm! The unicorn was hurt!

He might be a magical creature, but he was also an animal in trouble. Which meant they had to help.

She turned her bracelet three times.

There was a burst of magic from her wrist. It wasn't its usual gold, it was more of a straw-coloured yellow. But it drifted towards the unicorn and in a moment, the whickers and whinnies became words in her ears.

'Ouch, ouch, ouch,' the unicorn said.

'He's in pain,' Evie told Isabelle.

'So will Ryan be if we don't get help,'
Isabelle said anxiously.

Evie held Isabelle's hand, so that she could

understand the unicorn too. Isabelle's eyes widened in wonder.

'Isabelle,' Evie said, 'we have to try our best to help him. That's all we can do, but that's what we have to do. Are you ready to try your hardest?'

'That's what I said to you!' Isabelle said indignantly.

'I know. It was great advice,' Evie grinned.

They crept cautiously together towards the unicorn. His hooves were the size of dinner plates. His back was as broad as a table. He was huge. Ryan looked tiny crouched against the tree.

'Excuse me,' Evie said politely. 'Excuse me, please.'

The unicorn huffed. 'What? What do you want?'

Evie slid her feet carefully across the leaf litter, wary of making a single sudden sound. 'Please, could you let our friend Ryan go?'

'Go where?' the creature snorted.

'Anywhere,' Isabelle said, 'anywhere away from you!'

'Hush.' Evie didn't want the unicorn to be any angrier than he was already.

Isabelle snapped her mouth closed.

The clearing was still. The only sound was the busy chatter of birds in the bushes.

No. That wasn't the only sound.

There was giggling.

Definitely giggling – high-pitched like
a mosquito being tickled. She recognised
it and she felt a shiver run over her skin.
'Sprites,' she said.

'Where?' Isabelle's head whipped around,
desperate to see the little blue creatures.

'Close. Very close.'

'There.' Ryan said, as a tiny blue creature
crawled from under the unicorn's mane.
A tiny blue creature with wings and
pinching fingers.

Chapter 9

The sprite was perched on the unicorn's neck, giggling at them all.

'Unicorn,' Evie said, 'we're going to help you. Stay still, OK?'

The unicorn's tail twitched angrily. His hoof stomped, sending puffs of brown dust into the air. 'It hurts,' he snapped. 'It hurts!'

'I know, but if you can stay very still, I can try to take it off.'

The unicorn gave a whimper, but his legs stopped kicking and all four hooves stayed on the ground.

Evie edged closer. Now she could see dark beads of sweat on his coat. The muscles in his side rippled as he gasped. He was truly enormous.

The sprite swung across the unicorn's mane, using clumps of hair as ropes. It laughed as it went. Its wings were tucked tight to its body and Evie could see that its weight was pulling hard on the unicorn's hair.

'Let go!' she said sharply.

The sprite ignored her.

She reached up to try to pluck it from the unicorn, but it was completely out of her reach.

Ryan had edged away from the tree, now that the unicorn was still. 'Let me try,' he said. He reached up too, but his fingertips were nowhere near the unicorn's mane either.

'Ask the unicorn to kneel,' he whispered.

Good plan, she nodded. 'Excuse me, please, but would you mind bending down a little bit?' she asked the creature.

The unicorn didn't move. Had he heard her? Was he ignoring her?

'Excuse me?' She tapped him gently on his side.

He gave a series of quick whickers, neighs and whinnies.

But Evie couldn't understand a single thing he had said.

She twisted the bracelet sharply, pressing it into her skin. There was no gold light at all. She listened. The unicorn's insistent sounds made no sense to her.

What was happening?

Had Grandma Iris' gift broken?

No, not broken. Just worn off. She remembered the poem:

'All that glitters isn't gold,

Uncover magic, be brave, be bold.

Its power wanes on the third day.

Bark! Woof! Howl! What will you say?'

The bracelet had arrived three days ago. It wasn't supposed to last forever. It didn't work that way. Evie felt a stab of sadness. It was over. The magic was done.

But there wasn't time to get too upset – she could still see the sprite and it was still hurting the unicorn.

It was also still out of reach.

'Water bottles!' Isabelle yelled suddenly. 'The fox told you we wouldn't find the sprites near the lake because they don't like water!'

Ryan grinned at Isabelle, he understood. He flipped the lid off his bottle and sent a stream of water sailing towards the unicorn. It splashed the sprite from head to toe.

The little creature shook furiously and its giggle became a squeal.

Evie followed suit, squeezing her bottle hard.

Her stream crossed with Ryan's. Then Isabelle added to it. The stream became

a torrent for the sprite. It rose furiously, darting into the air with an angry shout. It rose higher, and higher, its wings spread and beating hard. Then it was lost among the rustling leaves of the sycamore.

The unicorn gave a gentle whinny.

'What did he say?' Isabelle asked eagerly – clearly delighted to have seen a sprite and a unicorn! It wasn't a normal sort of paper chase, that was for sure.

Evie slouched sadly. 'I don't know what he said. The bracelet has stopped working. There's no more magic.' She rested her hand on the unicorn's back, scratching it tenderly.

The unicorn whickered, then twirled its head. A warm swirl of golden light streamed from his horn and showered down delicate as dandelion clocks.

'The bracelet has stopped working,' the unicorn said, 'but that doesn't mean there's no more magic.'

'You can speak!' Isabelle said.

'Well, I *am* a unicorn. That's about as magical as you can be,' he said. 'Thank you for helping me. Those sprites are a horrible nuisance.'

They looked up to where the leaves rustled in the breeze, green hands waving down at them, but there was no sign of the blue sprite.

'Your grandma Iris has given you a rare gift,' the unicorn continued. 'There's magic everywhere, but most humans can't see it, and they certainly can't use it. But your grandma is special, and she hopes you will be too. I might be able to help you with that, seeing as you were kind enough to help me.'

He twirled his horn again and more gold showered on to them.

'That's a little thank you from me to you. You'll all be able to see magic wherever it is. But you'll have to wait for Grandma Iris to send you your next bracelet before you can use it again.'

Evie felt a rush of hope as she realised what the unicorn was saying. 'You mean there are more bracelets?'

'Oh, yes. Your grandma likes giving gifts.'

'How do you know all this?' Isabelle demanded with her hands on her hips.

'I am *still* a unicorn,' he replied.

From beyond the wood they could hear the sound of children shouting, calling to each other. The trail had gone cold and they were all seeking the hare.

The unicorn tossed his mane and plunged into the shadows of the rowan trees. With one last glint from his horn, he was gone.

It felt as though they were waking up from a deep sleep.

'Did that really happen?' Isabelle asked.

'I think so,' Evie replied.

'I think I'd better start running again,'
Ryan said.

'Yes, but keep away from the woods –
there are more sprites close by,' Evie
warned.

'Give me a ten-second head start, then the

race is back on!' Ryan cried. He whooped away, scattering a handful of paper like rain.

Isabelle counted to ten – quite quickly, Evie thought – then sprinted after him.

Chapter 10

In the park, all the runners were peering under benches and looking behind lamp-posts and around bins – where had the hare gone?

Then, Evie heard a yell as the trail was uncovered. She and Isabelle raced towards the noise. Everyone else was drawn in too,

coming from every direction like water
running down a plug hole.

She had to pace herself. She knew that
Ryan would want to lead them on a decent
run before heading back to the school yard.
She didn't want to run out of energy before
the last sprint.

Isabelle was at her side the whole way.
Around them were some of their classmates,
as well as some other children from lower
years. Evie felt her heart pulsing hard in
her chest, and her breathing became more
ragged as the race continued. The breeze
off the lake, as they ran past, was delicious.
Passing piles of white paper, like pale flowers
blooming at the edge of the path, was good

too – they were on the right track.

Ryan led them up towards the football fields, then up a steep grassy slope that Isabelle said was good for sledging in winter, then back towards the park entrance. One by one children began to drop behind.

Now, as they exited the park and headed back towards school, the parents had spilled out on to the street and were yelling them on. Evie felt her heart lift as she realised Isabelle had been right – everyone wanted her to do her best and their cries were encouraging her to do just that.

Which meant racing Isabelle.

As the school building came into view – the dark fortress walls and the black railings

like a knights' guard of honour – Evie
looked at Isabelle. Who was looking
right back.

'Race you!' Isabelle said.

With a yell, Evie broke into her fastest

sprint. Isabelle was right behind her.

Evie put everything she could into her run – all the joy at Grandma Iris' gift, the fear of the sprites, and the elation of knowing there was more to come. Everything she could think of went as fuel for this race.

But Isabelle was edging closer and closer.

The crowd roared their support for the two girls who were in the lead, and neck-and-neck.

Evie stretched out her hand, desperate to be the first one through the gates and into the yard. She leaned in to the finish.

But it was Isabelle who went through in front.

Parents, teachers, friends, all clapped with

joy for Isabelle. The winner herself had
dropped on to her back and was staring up
at the sky, her breathing quick and
her cheeks flushed. Evie dropped down
beside her.

Ryan leaned in over them both and
scattered the last of his confetti so that it
fell in a rain above them.

Evie giggled. She had tried her best, her very hardest, but Isabelle had won fair and square. 'I'll beat you next time,' she said with a grin.

She saw magic arc its way above the three of them, a rainbow of golden shades.

'Wow!' Isabelle said. 'Did you see that?'

'Yup,' Ryan agreed.

It was the unicorn's gift – all three of them were able to see magic. But Evie couldn't use it without help from Grandma Iris. She smiled. She could wait. There was more than enough fun in the world right now, even without the bracelet.

Later on, after hugging Dad, and him texting Mum and Nana Em, Evie walked on to the little stage that had been put up in the yard, to get her medal. Miss Williams smiled warmly at her. 'Evie Hall, you are a very welcome addition to our school,' she said lowering the ribbon over Evie's head. 'Let's hope that this excellent performance continues.'

Evie looked down, and, though the medal that hung from the ribbon was silver, she felt as though she had won gold.

Evie and friends

Evie

Full name: Evie Hall

Lives in: Sheffield

Family: Mum, Dad, younger sister Lily

Pets: Chocolate Labrador Myla and cat Luna

Favourite foods: rice, peas and chicken – lasagna – and chocolate bourbon biscuits!

Best thing about Evie: friendly and determined!

Isabelle

Full name: Isabelle Carter

Lives in: Sheffield

Family: Mum, Dad, older sister Lizzie

Favourite foods: sweet treats – and anything spicy!

Best thing about Isabelle: she's the life and soul of the party!

Ryan

Full name: Ryan Harris

Lives in: Sheffield

Family: lives with his mum, visits his dad

Pets: would love a dog …

Favourite foods: Marmite, chocolate – and anything with pasta!

Best thing about Ryan: easy-going, and fun to be with!

Who's your
Magic Bracelet
★ ☆ ♥ ☆ ♥ Best Friend?

Take this quiz to find out
who would be your BFF!

Do you love animals?

A. ❏ I love all animals. They're so CUTE!

B. ❏ They're OK, but I'd rather hang out
with my friends.

C. ❏ I think animals are great but I would
really like a dog most of all.

What's your favourite food?

A. ❏ It has to be a chocolate bourbon biscuit.

B. ❏ Anything from a fancy restaurant!

C. ❏ A picnic on the hills with my family.

Do you like being the centre of attention?

A. ❏ I'm not a huge fan of big crowds.

B. ❏ Yes of course, the more people the better!

C. ❏ I'm happy either way.

Which accessory couldn't you live without?

A. ❑ My bracelet!

B. ❑ Ooh, so many to choose from!
Though I could always do with one more …

C. ❑ Um … my water bottle?

If your friend is upset, what would you do to cheer them up?

A. ❑ Try to find out what the problem is.

B. ❑ Give them encouragement. I do a
great pep talk!

C. ❑ Distract them with a joke.

Mostly A
Your BFF
would be: **Evie**

Mostly B
Your BFF
would be: **Isabelle**

Mostly C
Your BFF
would be: **Ryan**

Can you find all the words?

EVIE   RYAN

UNICORN   GLITTERS

LUNA   BRACELET

SPRITES   MAGIC

ISABELLE   MYLA

B	R	A	C	E	L	E	T	H	P
J	Y	I	G	E	V	I	Q	K	O
I	A	A	L	A	T	I	E	S	L
U	N	H	I	R	F	U	E	H	U
N	N	A	T	L	Y	B	S	E	N
I	R	J	T	I	I	M	Y	L	A
C	U	L	E	E	E	A	L	L	M
O	H	A	R	S	D	G	D	E	R
R	M	E	S	P	R	I	T	E	S
N	I	M	T	C	S	C	E	R	H
I	M	I	S	A	B	E	L	L	E

Jessica Ennis-Hill grew up in Sheffield with her parents and younger sister. She has been World and European heptathlon champion and won gold at the London 2012 Olympics and silver at Rio 2016. She still lives in Sheffield and enjoys reading stories to her son every night.

You can find Jessica on Twitter **@J_Ennis**, on Facebook, and on Instagram **@jessicaennishill**

Jessica says: *'I have so many great memories of being a kid. My friends and I spent lots of time exploring and having adventures where my imagination used to run riot! It has been so much fun working with Elen Caldecott to go back to that world of stories and imagination. I hope you'll enjoy them too!'*

Elen Caldecott co-wrote the Evie's Magic Bracelet stories with Jessica. Elen lives in Totterdown, in Bristol – chosen mainly because of the cute name. She has written several warm, funny books about ordinary children doing extraordinary things.

You can find out more at www.elencaldecott.com